# DINOSAUR WORLD

Written by: Geoffrey T. Williams
Illustrated by: Wendy Huber

PRICE STERN SLOAN
Los Angeles

**Dinosaur World can be read with its accompanying word-for-word cassette to create a truly absorbing learning experience.**

Mary and her father are spending the morning at the zoo. The peacocks are strutting and cawing. The laughing kookaburras are chuckling to themselves. Suddenly, a lion's roar fills the air.

"He must be hungry," says Mary.

"Or maybe he's just bragging," says her father. "He's telling the whole jungle how brave he is."

"Just like the dinosaurs did."

"The dinosaurs?"

"Yeah, you know, Tyrannosaurus Rex and Pterodactyls."

"Yeah, I know. But how do you know what it sounded like a million years ago?"

"I went to Dinosaur World last year with my class."

"Dinosaur World. Yeah, I remember that. Was that fun?"

"You haven't been there yet?"

"Not yet."

Mary starts to get excited, "Why don't we go now?"

Dad looks at his watch, "Well, I don't know if we have..."

"Come on. We don't have to meet Mom for a couple of hours."

"Yeah...but I..."

"And we could have a hot dog on the way..."

Well, of course, Dad can't resist that.

"And you can have mustard..."

"Okay."

And off to Dinosaur World they go.

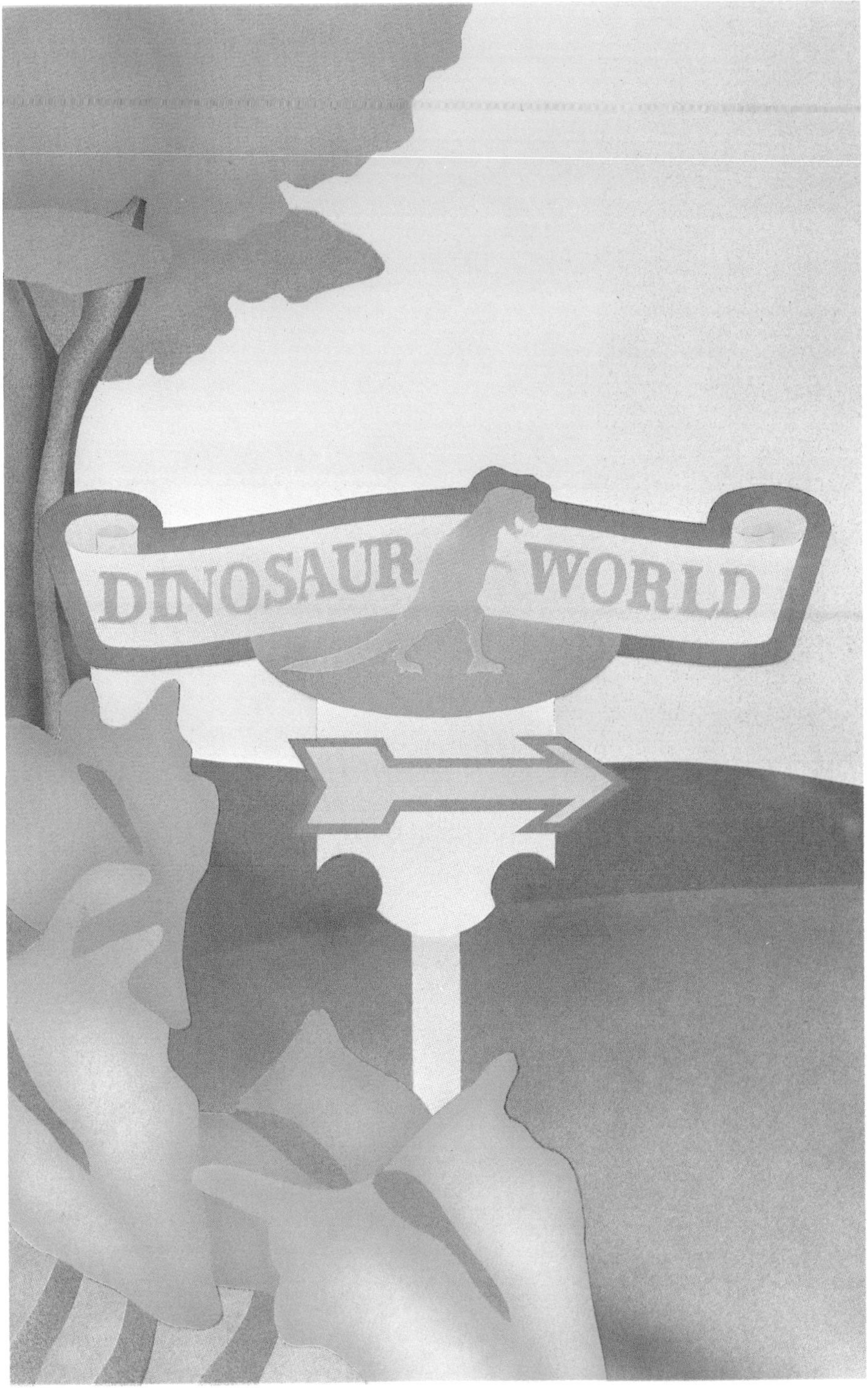
DINOSAUR WORLD

As Mary and her father get to Dinosaur World they see that many things look different. There are plants that look like giant ferns, with thick leaves that droop down. There's a smudge of smoke rising above the trees from a small volcano. They can hear it erupting. There are flying creatures overhead that don't quite look like birds. But some things remain the same. There is still a ticket window.

"Welcome to Dinosaur World," says the girl at the window.

"Thanks." Dad pays the admission.

"We'll need one of those tour radios," says Mary.

"Here you are." The girl hands them a small portable radio with a thin antenna. Then she reads from the Official Dinosaur World Guide Book, "Observe all posted regulations, stay on the marked paths and, for your own safety . . ."

"Don't feed the dinosaurs," they join in.

Just as they begin walking along the path, dozens of little animals run by. Mary and her father hop about on tip-toe, laughing and trying to keep out of their way.

"They're all over!"

"There's one on my shoe!"

"They must be some kind of dinosaur."

"But, they're smaller than a chicken!" Dad shouts.

Suddenly, a small voice is heard. "The small dinosaurs running loose throughout Dinosaur World are Compsognathus, which means pretty jaw."

Dad is startled. "Wait a minute! Who said that?"

"I did."

Mary points to the tour radio, "It's the radio, Dad."

The voice continues, "They lived during the Jurassic period about 150 million years ago. And though they are carnivorous..."

"That means they eat meat," explains Mary.

"...they're much too small to bother with people," the radio says.

A little further down the path they hear the sound of waves breaking on a rocky beach. And as they round the bend Mary points, "That's the ocean."

"It's not really the ocean," explains their radio guide. "It's a reproduction of the great Inland Sea that spread across the mid-western states of North America. We call it Dinosaur Sea."

Just then, a tremendous screech is heard.

"Is that a bird?" Dad wants to know.

"No, that's a Pteranadon. See, he doesn't have any feathers."

Seeing their leathery wings Dad says, "Like a bat."

"The Pteranadons and Pterodactyls live on the cliffs bordering the Dinosaur Sea. And even though the average wingspan is twenty-seven feet . . ."

Dad is amazed. "Twenty-seven feet!"

". . . they don't weigh much more than a big Thanks-giving turkey. About 30 pounds."

Mary points to the cliffs, "Here comes another one!"

"Wow!"

And they both watch as the graceful Pteranadon skims just above the waves, occasionally dipping its giant beak into the water to catch a fish.

A big flipper pokes above the waves, followed by the head and finally the whole shell of a huge sea creature.

"Look, Dad. See that giant turtle?"

"Uh-huh."

Mary points to the Archelon, "That weighs more than an elephant."

"Wow!"

"And see right there?"

"A giant crocodile!"

"It's the ancestor of modern crocodiles," the radio tells them, "a Tylosaurus."

Suddenly the sea is churned up as the ancient enemies battle one another.

The Archelon is lucky. He escapes this time. As he swims away Dad tells Mary, "You know, I bet if we went over to that swampy area, that we could see some different kinds of dinosaurs."

As Mary and her father can see, the swamp is the home for many familiar creatures, like frogs, ducks and gulls, as well as strange looking dinosaurs.

Mary says to her dad, "They like the plants that grow here."

"Oh. What are those big spotted ones? The ones eating over there?" Dad wants to know.

"Iguanodons. And they were found all over the world."

"Oh. Because back then all the continents were connected."

Mary is surprised. "No oceans?"

"Well, sure. Just not like today. It was more like one great big ocean."

They watch as the slow-moving creatures tear at leaves and small branches, chewing just like cows.

"Look!" shouts Dad.

"A family of duckbills," Mary says as their guide explains, "A small herd of Lambeosaurus Duckbills lives near the swamp. The large hatchet-shaped crest on top of the head is hollow and perhaps helped distinguish one type of duckbill from another."

Mary points to the biggest one, "That one's as long as a bus!"

"Listen. During mating season they trumpet to each other."

Of course, one of the most famous of all dinosaurs also lives by the swamp.

"A Brontosaurus!" says Dad.

But the radio corrects him, "Scientists have changed his name to Apatosaurus."

"He's taller than our house!"

"He's one of our most popular attractions. He likes visitors too. And, if you're lucky he'll come over to look at you."

Just at that moment the giant beast swings his head towards his visitors and they can hear him breathing.

"Despite growing over 70 feet long. . ."

"70 feet long!" Dad is amazed.

". . .Apatosaurus only weighs about as much as 10 elephants," the radio continues. "His long neck lets him browse high in the treetops for food. And he spends at least a part of his time in the water."

"I bet if that tail of his ever got started . . ." And, sure enough, just as Dad says it, there goes the beast's massive tail. Branches crack and trees fall to the ground.

"He probably uses that tail to defend himself from the big meat-eaters."

"Now, let's go see the Tyrannosaurus Rex," says Mary.

As they head past the swamp and leave Dinosaur Sea behind, several animals gallop past, running on their long hind legs. Dad is impressed. "Wow! That's fast! What kind is that?"

Mary knows. "An ostrich dinosaur, called Dromiceiomimus, I think."

"Right again," says the radio. "The Dromiceiomimus is the fastest of all dinosaurs."

"I bet!"

"He grows to over 11 feet long, including his tail, which he uses for balance. He could probably run faster than any horse and he had eyes bigger than any animal alive today."

"Hear that?" asks Mary as a loud cracking sound is heard in the distance.

"Sounds like deer crashing their antlers together."

"There they are," Mary points. As they get closer, they can see the animals charging at one another.

"Ow! That's gotta hurt."

"It wouldn't if your skull was that thick. They're Bone-heads."

"Pachycephalosaurus," says the radio.

"Easy for you to say," laughs Dad.

"Their skulls are over 10 inches thick. See the other ones grazing over there?"

"No. . ."

"Over there by those big tree ferns."

Dad sees them. "Oh, yeah. Sure."

"Well, the winner of the fight will probably rule that herd."

"Just like deer and wild sheep."

A ferocious looking creature lumbers into view. "Spinosaurus!" says Mary.

"'Cause of that sail on his back, right?" asks her father.

"Probably."

"The Spinosaurus, a flesh-eating dinosaur from Egypt in the late Cretaceous, has a huge skin sail along his back."

"Wonder why?"

"Well, since most scientists think dinosaurs were cold-blooded reptiles," the radio explains, "Spinosaurus might have used his sail to regulate body heat by turning toward, or away from the sun."

"Sure!" says Dad. "If he turns sideways, more sun hits the sail and he gets hotter and if he faces the sun, less light hits it and he cools down."

"Very good."

"Thanks!"

"They grow to be up to 40 feet long and they weigh about 7 tons."

"That's about, uh, what? Two and a half elephants?"

"Now can we see the Tyrannosaurus Rex?" Mary wants to know.

"We're almost there."

As they leave the clearing they come to a large fenced pasture area and Dinosaur World's newest and most exciting exhibit.

"What's that cloud of dust?" Mary wants to know.

"And that sound," says her dad. "It's like a cattle stampede."

"Yeah. What is it?"

"It's a whole herd. . ."

"Of Triceratops! But why are they running?"

Her father points across the field. "I think I see why."

"A Tyrannosaurus Rex!"

"The tyrant-lizard," says their radio. "Probably the most ferocious carnivore that ever lived. Tyrannosaurus is almost 40 feet long and 18 feet tall."

"His head's bigger than my whole body!" shouts Mary.

"Is he after Triceratops?"

"It sure looks like it. But he's in for a fight."

The radio tells them, "Triceratops is twice as big as a rhinoceros, and has those huge horns over three feet long. Most of the time they just browse and graze in quiet herds like cattle."

"There they go!"

It's not long after the exciting fight when they decide it's time to leave.

"Getting tired?"

"A little," admits Mary. "But it was sure fun."

"Yeah. Thanks for bringing me."

"See you next time," the radio calls after them.

"Where do you suppose all the real dinosaurs went?"

"They all died millions of years ago," Mary tells him.

"How come?"

"Well, scientists think that a huge meteor hit the earth and blew up dust that made the sun too dim."

"I bet that killed the plants that the dinosaurs ate too."

"And made the weather too cold."

But Dad is a little doubtful, "But are they sure that's what happened?"

"Well, not positive. But they keep looking for the answers."

"Have you ever thought about helping them out?"

"Maybe when I get a little older, Dad."